DANCE DILEMMA

text by Leigh McDonald
illustrated by Katie Wood

Raintree is an imprint of Capstone Global Library Limited, a company incorporated in England and Wales having its registered office at 264 Banbury Road, Oxford, OX2 7DY – Registered company number: 6695582

www.raintree.co.uk
myorders@raintree.co.uk

Graphic Designer: Kristi Carlson
Production Specialist: Laura Manthe
Illustrated by Katie Wood
Originated by Capstone Global Library Ltd
Printed and bound in China

ISBN 978 1 4747 3231 4
20 19 18 17 16
10 9 8 7 6 5 4 3 2 1

British Library Cataloguing in Publication Data
A full catalogue record for this book is available from the British Library.

Every effort h been made to
reproduced in
printings if n

CONTENTS

Dance Team
TRYOUTS

Chapter one

A NEW ROUTINE

As Hannah walked out of her English class at Milton Secondary School, a poster across the crowded corridor caught her eye. She grabbed her best friend, Caitlin, and dragged her over for a closer look.

"Cool! Dance squad trials!" Hannah said. "We have to do this! Last year they won the local championships with that 'I've Got A Feeling' routine, remember?"

"That was awesome!" Caitlin agreed.

The girls studied the poster. It was covered with photos of the dance squad performing at competitions and events.

"That looks awesome," Caitlin said. "Count me in!"

"Auditions are in two weeks," Hannah read from the poster. "Want to come over tonight and practise at my house?"

"Sure! Do you think they'll let us audition together?" Hannah asked.

"I don't know," Caitlin said. "But we can at least practise together. Maybe we can look at some videos online for ideas tonight and pick a routine to copy."

"That's a great idea," Hannah said. "I can't wait! This is going to be so much fun!"

* * *

After school, Hannah and Caitlin rode their bikes to Hannah's house. Hannah rushed inside and told her mum about the upcoming dance team trials.

"That sounds like a great idea, girls," Hannah's mum said. "Let me know if you need any help. I did a little bit of dancing in college, you know."

"Thanks, Mum," Hannah said. "We'll let you know. We're going to go find a song for our routine." She grabbed Caitlin's arm, and they rushed to Hannah's room to get started.

Hannah searched online and found hundreds of videos of dance teams performing. Some of them were really fast and complicated. Luckily, they found several routines that didn't look too hard for beginners.

Caitlin and Hannah decided on a routine that was set to a popular hip-hop song. They watched the first few moves over and over online.

"Okay, let's try running through the beginning," Hannah suggested.

She and Caitlin pushed her bed against the wall to create an open space. They tried to copy what they'd seen in the video, starting with a high kick followed by a spin. Then they criss-crossed their legs and spun in the other direction before windmilling their arms and spinning to the ground.

"That was easy!" Caitlin said. She reached out to hit play on the video.

"I don't know," Hannah said, frowning. "Does it look right when I do the spin? It feels kind of awkward."

"You look fine," Caitlin said. "Let's watch the next part."

The girls spent the next hour going over the routine. Caitlin seemed to pick all the moves up easily. But Hannah wasn't so sure. She still felt like she was having trouble keeping up.

Good thing I have two weeks before the trials, Hannah thought. *I'm going to need it.*

Chapter two

TRIALS

Hannah and Caitlin practised together almost every day for the next two weeks. Caitlin seemed totally confident, but Hannah was still a little nervous.

Finally the day of the trials arrived. Hannah and Caitlin went to the gym after school and took seats in the stands with some other girls. After they waited for a few minutes, a woman walked in wearing a Milton Secondary School Dance Squad T-shirt.

"Hi, everyone. I'm Erica, the dance squad coach," she began. "First of all, I want to thank you all for coming today. I'm excited to see so many new faces at trials."

Erica held up a piece of paper. "I need everyone who's trying out to put their name on this sign-up sheet," she instructed. "We'll start off by running through some basic warm-ups together. Then I'll call you up for individual auditions."

She motioned to a young guy standing near the speaker system. "Give your music to Josh when it's your turn," she said.

All the dancers jumped up from their spots in the stands and ran over to sign up. Caitlin was third on the sign-up sheet. Since they'd be trying out individually, Hannah was fourth.

Miss Erica had everyone practise some basic dance techniques like toe touches, turns and leaps as a group. When they'd finished warming up, the first girl took her place in the centre of the floor. The rest of the dancers sat in the stands to watch.

It was exciting to watch the other girls perform. Everyone seemed like they really knew their routines. When it was Caitlin's turn, she performed flawlessly. Hannah clapped loudly for her friend when she finished.

The coach looked down at the sign-up sheet. "Hannah, you're up next," she called loudly.

Hannah's stomach did a nervous flip-flop. *Oh, no*, she thought. *What if I screw this up?*

Hannah stood up and handed her CD to the boy running the music. Then she took her place in front of the judging table. Miss Erica sat there with two other girls. Hannah recognised them as senior members of the dance team.

As the music started, Hannah crossed her left leg behind her right. Then she realised she had started on the wrong foot! It took her a few beats to get her routine back on track. She spent the rest of the routine trying not to let the mistake throw her off. But it was hard. She was a beat behind the music and felt embarrassed.

"Great job, Hannah," Miss Erica said when the music ended.

Hannah smiled nervously and took her seat in the stands to watch the rest of trials.

When everyone finished, Miss Erica stood up and faced the stands. "I want to thank you all again for coming here today," she said. "Everyone did a great job. Please check the notice board outside my office for the results tomorrow after school."

* * *

The next day, Hannah could barely focus in any of her classes. All she could think about was whether or not she'd made the squad.

What if Caitlin made it and I didn't? Hannah thought.

When the final bell rang, Hannah rushed down to the gym. Caitlin was already there, right in the middle of the crowd of girls gathered around the notice board.

Hannah pushed to the centre of the group and stood on her toes, trying to see the notice board. But before she could finish reading the list, Caitlin grabbed her and hugged her.

"We made it! We both made it!" she heard Caitlin exclaim.

Hannah looked at the list. Sure enough, down near the bottom, there was her name! She jumped up and down, and threw her arms around Caitlin.

"This is going to be the best year ever!" Hannah said.

Chapter three

FIRST PRACTICE

The dance squad's first practice was scheduled for Monday after school. Hannah and Caitlin walked to the changing room together after their final class and quickly changed into their practice uniforms. Then they joined the rest of the team on the gym floor.

Miss Erica walked to the centre of the floor. She clapped her hands to get the girls' attention.

"Welcome, girls," she said. "Take a look around you, and get to know your new family! Some of you are familiar faces, and some are joining us for the very first time. But we're all going to come together over the next few weeks to form a great dance squad. Are you ready?"

"Yeah!" all of the girls shouted. Everyone sounded excited to get started.

"Spread out and take a spot, everyone," Miss Erica said. "We'll start with some stretching and warm-ups first."

The girls all spread out on mats on the gym floor to stretch. Hannah sat down in the middle with the soles of her feet touching and her arms extended straight out in front of her. She leaned forwards and arched her back, stretching out the muscles along her spine.

Then she extended her arms and legs straight out in front of her. She reached her arms long towards her ankles. Hannah could feel the stretch along the backs of her legs in her hamstrings.

After they'd finished stretching on the mats, the coach had them work on some cardio exercises to get their heart rates up.

Hannah loved the feeling of getting her body moving and her blood pumping. By the time the coach turned on the music, Hannah couldn't wait to dance.

The first couple of moves they worked on were simple. Soon everyone was moving in sync. Then the coach showed them a longer sequence with a spin in it. Several of the girls lost their balance. They tried it a few times, but it wasn't coming together.

"Caitlin," Miss Erica said, "you have the routine down perfectly. Can you come up here and show us?"

Caitlin walked up to the front of the group and got into position. She easily performed the moves they'd learned so far, starting with the leap across the floor and ending with the spin. She made it look so easy.

"Thank you, Caitlin. That looked great," said Miss Erica. "Okay, everyone, let's try it again."

This time, the whole team made it through the sequence together – except Hannah. She just couldn't quite manage to spin gracefully. She kept coming out her spin a beat too late and missing the following step.

"Geez," she heard an older girl mutter. "How'd she make the team?"

"This is only our first practice," Miss Erica reassured everyone. "You're all doing great! I want everyone to go home and practise what we've learned today. I think we'll see a great improvement next time. Now go and get cleaned up, and I'll see everyone back here on Thursday."

Hannah was quiet. It seemed like everyone on the team was a better dancer than she was. If she didn't improve, she didn't know how long her time on the dance squad would last.

Chapter four

PULLED IN TWO DIRECTIONS

After she got dressed, Hannah headed down the hall to talk to Miss Erica in her office. "Coach?" she said tentatively from the doorway. "Do you have a minute?"

"Of course I do. Come in, Hannah," Miss Erica said, smiling. "What's on your mind?"

Hannah came in and sat down at the desk. She fidgeted with her skirt a bit, not sure how to begin.

"I'm really excited to be a part of the dance squad," Hannah finally said. "But I'm worried that I'm going to mess everyone else up. I was having some trouble with the routine today."

"You're doing fine, Hannah," Miss Erica assured her. "It was your first day! You just need to spend some time practising. Once you get used to the moves they'll come more naturally."

"Can you give me some things I can practise at home?" Hannah said.

The coach gave her a couple of videos and an exercise notebook.

"I think you'll feel much more confident once we go through the routine and you get more comfortable with the steps," Miss Erica told her.

* * *

Hannah called Caitlin when she got home and told her about meeting with the coach. "Want to come over and practise with me?" Hannah asked.

"Okay, I guess," Caitlin said. "I'll be there in an hour."

Hannah changed into her workout clothes and waited for Caitlin to arrive. When the doorbell rang, she hurried to the door to open it. Caitlin stood on the porch, wearing her normal clothes.

"Hey," Hannah said. "You're going to dance in that?"

"Well, Becca texted me, and she's going to see a film tonight," Caitlin explained. "I thought maybe we could do that instead. I mean, we just had practice today."

"Yeah, but I really need more practice," Hannah said. She led Caitlin to her bedroom. "Did you see me trying to do the spin sequence? It was so embarrassing! I need to get it right before Thursday. You had it perfect. Can you help me?"

"Sure," Caitlin said. "It's simple. Here, watch." She quickly ran through the steps.

But when Hannah tried to do the spin, she almost fell over.

"Try it again, and when you spin, look at one spot so you don't get dizzy," Caitlin said. "That's what they do in ballet."

Hannah tried again, fixing her eyes on the window as she spun. This time she hit the next step right on target.

"Hey!" she said. "Thanks! That helped a lot!" She ran through the steps again.

"Awesome," Caitlin said. "You look way better. Now can we go to the cinema?"

"Well, I just figured this out," Hannah said. "I want to run through it some more and really get it down. Plus I have these tapes Miss Erica gave me. I wanted to watch them."

Caitlin sighed and stood up. "Well, I told Becca that I'd go to the cinema with her," she said. "Are you sure you don't want to come?"

"No," Hannah said. "I really want to get this perfect."

"Okay. I'll see you tomorrow, then, I guess," Caitlin said. She shrugged as she walked out the door.

Chapter five

SOLO SPOTS

Hannah made sure to get to practice extra early. She wanted to make sure she had time to warm up before everyone else arrived. She was already out on the gym floor, stretching, when the coach walked in.

"Hey there, early bird," Miss Erica called from the doorway. "How have those practice videos been working out for you?"

"Great!" Hannah said. "They're really helping. I feel a lot better now."

"Keep up the good work!" Miss Erica told her. "I can't wait to see what you've learned at practice today."

The other girls trailed in and took their spots on the floor. Caitlin gave Hannah's ponytail a friendly tug as she walked over and sat down beside her to stretch.

"Everyone take a seat," Miss Erica called. "I have a couple of announcements to make before we get started."

She held up a slip of paper. "Our invitation to the regional competition just came," she said. "We're going to spend the next two weeks practising our routine with rotating positions. At the end of those two weeks, we'll hold trials for three solo spots. That way, you'll all have a chance to learn all the moves and prepare if you decide to go for a solo. Any questions?"

Hannah raised her hand. "Do we need to come up with a performance for the trials?" she asked.

"Good question," Miss Erica said. "I'll have you all run through the solo spots for the competition routine. No one needs to come up with anything new. I want everyone to be focused on learning the competition routine."

There was lots of excited chatter as the coach walked over to her MP3 player and started the music. An upbeat medley of '80s music came on.

Miss Erica did a quick run-through of the performance. She started crouched on the ground before slowly rolling her body up to a standing position. When she reached the top, she stuck her left leg out to the side and pirouetted across the gym floor.

She makes it look so easy, Hannah thought as she watched Miss Erica demonstrate the routine.

When the coach was done, the girls took positions and started working. A lot of the steps were harder than the stuff they'd been working on so far.

Hannah could tell that the routine was going to look awesome. But the changes in tempo between the songs were going to take some getting used to.

As they practised, Hannah looked around at her team members. *I wonder who's thinking of trying out for a solo*, she thought. *I wonder if I could get one.*

Hannah wasn't sure she could compete with some of the more experienced dancers. Was it worth trying?

Chapter six

A LONG AFTERNOON

In the changing room after practice, one of the other dancers, a girl named Emily, came up to Hannah.

"You looked great out there, Hannah," Emily said. "Are you going to try out for one of the solos?"

"Maybe," Hannah replied. "Are you?"

"I don't know," Emily replied. "I'm thinking about it. I just wonder how many people are going to be trying out."

Just then Caitlin walked up. "Want to come shopping with me?" she asked. "I finally saved enough to buy those red boots!"

Hannah glanced over at Emily. "I don't know," she began. "I have to write an English essay tonight. And I really wanted to have time to get some extra practice in, so. . ."

"Please?" Caitlin said. "We haven't been shopping together in ages! It won't kill you to have some fun, too, you know."

Caitlin looked so hopeful that Hannah couldn't refuse. "Okay," she said finally. "Just let me call my mum."

"Yay!" Caitlin said happily. She linked arms with Hannah and pulled her out the door.

As soon as they got to the shopping centre, Caitlin made a beeline for her favourite stop and bought the red boots. She ran over to a bench and immediately put them on.

"They look awesome," Hannah said.

"Thanks! Hey, let's go see who's at the arcade," Caitlin suggested. She walked off towards the gaming area.

Hannah hesitated. She really needed to get home to practise, but she didn't want Caitlin to be upset with her. Finally she ran to catch up with her friend.

Inside the dark arcade, there were a few kids playing video games. Hannah didn't recognise anybody. Then she felt Caitlin elbow her. Hannah turned to see where she was looking.

Connor Beale, a boy from school, stood in the back corner playing a video game. Caitlin had been talking about Connor nonstop since they'd worked on a big project together in English class.

"Do you think I should go over?" Caitlin asked in a whisper. She didn't wait for an answer. "I'm going over."

Hannah followed Caitlin as she walked over and said hello to Connor. She quickly became interested in how to play the game and started asking Connor lots of questions.

Hannah sighed and sat down on a nearby bench. She watched Caitlin flip her hair and giggle at something Connor said.

I wish I hadn't told Mum that I'd get a ride home from Caitlin's mum, Hannah thought. *It's going to be a long afternoon.*

Chapter seven

NEW FRIENDS

The next day, Hannah couldn't stop yawning. She'd got home from the shopping centre just in time for dinner and stayed up late to finish all of her homework. She hadn't done any dancing at all.

At practice that afternoon, Hannah felt sluggish, like she was dancing underwater. The coach had to correct her twice when she forgot the steps in part of the routine. The more mistakes she made, the worse she felt.

Caitlin, on the other hand, was dancing as well as always. It was her turn to stand in for the lead solo, and she was hitting all the steps. She didn't seem to be at all tired from the day before.

"Do you think you're going to try out for a solo?" Hannah asked Caitlin in the changing room after practice.

Caitlin looked in the mirror, pulling her hair into a ponytail. She shrugged carelessly. "Yeah, I guess I'll probably try out. The solos aren't really hard, anyway," she said.

"I might try out, too," Hannah said, glancing at Caitlin in the mirror to see her reaction.

Caitlin smiled. "That's great!" she said. "You should."

"Do you want to come over and practise on Saturday?" Hannah asked. "I want to run through the solos at home a few times before I have to dance in front of the whole squad."

Caitlin frowned. "I don't know," she said. "I don't really think I need to practise this weekend. I might go to Funscape with my sister. Do you want to come?"

"No, thanks," Hannah said. She was disappointed. She'd really been hoping her best friend could help her practise.

Just then, Emily walked over. "Did I hear you say you're trying out for a solo?" she asked.

"Yeah," Hannah answered. "Caitlin is busy on Saturday, but do you want to come over and practise with me?"

"Definitely!" Emily said, "That sounds like fun! Can we invite Abby, too?"

"Of course," Hannah said. She followed Emily to talk to a tall girl standing nearby. By the time they were done making plans, Caitlin was gone.

At home, Hannah told her mother about the solo tryouts. "Is it okay if I have a couple of friends over to practise?" she asked.

"Of course! I'm so proud of you for putting so much work into this," her mum said, giving her a hug. "I can't wait to see you dancing up on that stage!"

Chapter eight

PRACTICE MAKES PERFECT

On Saturday Emily and Abby came over to practise. Hannah had cleared an area in the front room for them to practise. She'd also brought down her MP3 player and some snacks.

"Great practice room!" Emily said. "I usually have to practise outside at my house. Otherwise I have to dance around my brother and his friends." She rolled her eyes.

Hannah laughed. "I usually practise in my room," she admitted. "But I thought with all three of us here, we'd need more space."

Hannah turned on the music, and the girls worked on the routine. They each took a turn performing their solos. They were having so much fun that they didn't even notice when Hannah's mum came and sat on the stairs to watch them. After a run-through with Hannah dancing the lead solo, her mum started clapping.

"Mum! How long have you been there?" Hannah asked in surprise.

"Long enough," her mum said. "That was great! I can't believe how much stronger and faster you are now than when you first started dancing. All that practice is really paying off!"

Hannah's mum smiled at Emily and Abby. "Are you having fun?" she asked.

"Yes," Emily said. "Thank you for letting us practise here!"

"My pleasure," Hannah's mother replied, before leaving them to it. "You girls are welcome anytime."

* * *

At Monday's practice after school, Hannah walked in with Abby. They were deep in conversation about a high school dance competition that had taken place over the weekend. They'd both seen the winning team's routine online.

"Can you believe how good they were?" Abby said. "I can't imagine how long it must have taken them to learn that routine!"

"I know!" Hannah said, shaking her head. "Just thinking about our competition is enough for me!"

Just then, Caitlin came out of the changing room and joined them on the floor. She looked confused and a little hurt.

"I couldn't find you anywhere at lunch," she said to Hannah. "Where were you?"

"Oh, sorry," Hannah told her. "I was so busy practising this weekend that I got behind on some of my homework. I had to finish a maths assignment during lunch. How was Funscape? Did you go?"

"Yes!" Caitlin said. "Connor was there with some friends. But my sister totally embarrassed me! She spilled a whole drink all over the table and got everyone soaking wet and sticky. It was such a disaster!"

"Oh, no!" Hannah said. "Did he say anything to you today?"

Before Caitlin could answer, Miss Erica came in and clapped her hands for everyone to take their places.

"I just wanted to remind everyone that there are only two more practices before solo trials," she said. "Everyone take your spots. Hannah, why don't you dance the first solo today?"

Hannah couldn't believe it was finally her turn. But she couldn't wait. She knew she was ready.

Chapter nine

MAKING A CHOICE

The day before the solo trials, Hannah met Caitlin at her locker after school. She could see her friend grinning as she walked up.

I wonder what she's so excited about, Hannah thought.

"Connor invited me to hang out at his house tonight!" Caitlin said as soon as Hannah got close. "He's having some friends over, too. You have to come with me! Will your mum let you go?"

Hannah grew quiet. She knew her mother trusted her and would let her go if she asked, but the truth was that she didn't want to. She knew she needed to practise. If she went with Caitlin, she wouldn't get anything done. Saying that her mother wouldn't let her go would be a good excuse, but it would also be a lie. She shouldn't have to lie to her best friend.

"Hello? Earth to Hannah! Can you come or not? I need you!" Caitlin said. She stopped and stared at Hannah.

"The trials for solos are tomorrow," Hannah said slowly. "I've been working really hard on the routine, and I really want to do well. Even if I don't get a spot, I want to know I did my best. If I go out tonight and stay out late, there's no way I'll do a good job at trials tomorrow."

Caitlin looked angry. "You care more about the stupid dance squad than you care about me!" she snapped.

"That's not true!" Hannah protested.

"The old Hannah would have been excited that the boy I've liked forever is finally asking me to hang out," Caitlin said. "You can't think about anything except dance, dance, dance!"

"Caitlin, that's not fair! I–" Hannah started to say, but Caitlin cut her off.

"Forget it," she said, slamming her locker shut. "Just forget I even asked!"

Hannah couldn't believe it. *It's like she cares more about some boy than me,* she thought.

Chapter ten

IN THE SPOTLIGHT

The next day at school, Hannah couldn't stop thinking about her fight with Caitlin. She'd texted her friend "I'm sorry," but Caitlin hadn't written back.

When the final bell rang, Hannah went down to the gym to get ready for solo trials. She was the first to arrive and sat down on one of the mats to start stretching. Caitlin came in last and sat down in the back, looking tired.

Miss Erica arrived with the list of girls who would be trying out for solos. "Please have a seat in the stands," she instructed. "I'll call the girls trying out for solos one at a time."

Hannah watched as the first girl took her place on the floor. The girl, Megan, had been on the team for three years, and really knew her stuff. She made the solo routine look easy. Everybody in the stands clapped when she finished.

"Well done, Megan! Thank you," Miss Erica said. "Hannah? Are you ready?"

Hannah swallowed hard. She wasn't looking forwards to following such a great dancer, but she didn't have a choice.

I can do this, she thought. *I know the routine. I've had plenty of practice.*

Hannah walked to the centre of the floor and took a deep breath. She tried to clear her mind of everything but the routine. The music came on, and she listened to the eight-count beat as she launched into her routine.

Hannah did a cross-leg walk sideways across the gym floor, keeping time with the music. As her walk ended, she lifted her right leg in a high kick and threw her arms overhead into a V.

Coming down, she went immediately into a tight spin on her right foot. Hannah focused on one spot as she came out of her spin so she wouldn't lose her balance.

As soon as she finished spinning one direction, she turned and spun back the other way. Then she turned and did a leap across the gym floor.

Hannah was so focused on what she was doing that she forgot about everyone watching. As the music came to an end, she arched her back and let her head drop back behind her.

The rest of the dancers cheered, bringing Hannah back to the present. She grinned as she walked back towards the stands. Several girls leaned over to tell her what a great job she'd done.

Caitlin's name was called next. Hannah was nervous for her friend. Caitlin looked really tired. She was normally a graceful and energetic dancer, but her routine that day was sluggish. She even missed a step towards the end.

Hannah wanted to go over and hug her friend, but Caitlin sat back down at the far end of the stand by herself.

After the final girl finished her routine, Miss Erica took the floor again. "Thanks to all the girls who tried out today," she said. "You all did a great job. I won't keep you in suspense any longer. The lead solo in this year's regional competition will be performed by Megan," she announced.

Everyone clapped and cheered.

"The secondary solos will go to Emily and Hannah," Miss Erica continued. "Congratulations, girls! You all did an excellent job."

Emily squealed and threw her arms around Hannah, jumping up and down with excitement.

Hannah was in shock. She couldn't believe she'd done it! She was going to dance a solo!

Chapter eleven

FRIENDS AGAIN

On the bus that afternoon, Hannah sat down next to Emily and pulled out a book.

Caitlin leaned over and tapped Emily on the shoulder. "Do you mind if we switch seats?" she asked. "I want to talk to Hannah."

Emily looked over at Hannah, who nodded. "Of course," Emily said, standing up to make room. Caitlin plopped down in the seat with a grateful smile.

"Congratulations on your solo," Caitlin said. "You really deserved it."

"Thanks, Cait," Hannah said. She was a little surprised. She'd thought her friend was still mad. "I wish you'd got one, too."

Caitlin shook her head. "It's okay," she said. "I didn't really want it enough. The right people are in those spots."

"What happened, anyway?" Hannah asked.

Caitlin sighed. "I stayed out too late at Connor's house, and my parents grounded me," she said. "I was so sleepy and so mad that I couldn't focus. I really messed things up. And I really missed you," she added sadly. "Connor played video games with his friends the whole time. I could have really used a friend to talk to."

"I missed you, too," Hannah said, giving her friend a hug. "I'm sorry I wasn't there for you when you needed me. I know how long you've liked Connor."

"It's okay," Caitlin said. "You were right. The dance squad is important to you. I get that. And all that extra practice paid off! Maybe you can even show me some of your moves."

"Definitely," Hannah said. "You can come over and dance with me. I've got a great practice space set up."

"That would be fun," Caitlin said, grinning. "We can try some of those fancy moves I saw them do at the high school regionals."

"You watched the high school regionals?" Hannah said.

"Sure," Caitlin said. "It was posted online this weekend. Did you see it? They did some crazy routines!"

"Yeah! That Michael Jackson routine the winning team did? With the flips?" Hannah squealed. "And what about that guy on their team? Really cute, right?"

"So cute," Caitlin said, sighing.

Hannah grinned. She'd got a solo, and she'd gotten her friend back. Joining the dance squad was turning out to be more fun than she'd expected. She couldn't wait to see how they did at regionals.

AUTHOR BIO

Leigh McDonald loves books! Whether she's writing them, reading them, editing them or designing their covers, books are what she does best. She lives in a colourful bungalow in Tucson, Arizona, USA, with her husband, Porter, her daughter, Adair, and two big, crazy dogs named Roscoe! and Rosie.

ILLUSTRATOR BIO

Katie Wood fell in love with drawing when she was very small. Since graduating from Loughborough University School of Art and Design in 2004, she has been living her dream working as a freelance illustrator. From her studio in Leicester, England, she creates bright and lively illustrations for books and magazines all over the world.

GLOSSARY

competition contest of some kind

complicated something that contains many different parts or ideas and is difficult to use or understand

focus to concentrate on something

performance public presentation of a play, movie or piece of music

routine set of moves a dancer performs

sequence following of one thing after another in a fixed order

sluggish moving slowly and lacking in energy

solo performance done by a single person

COMPREHENSION QUESTIONS

1. Have you ever had to audition for something? What was it? Talk about what you did to prepare.

2. Hannah practises with some other members of the dance team when Caitlin is too busy. How do you think this made Caitlin feel? Talk about it.

3. Hannah and Caitlin are best friends, but they have a fight. Who do you think was right? Talk about what it means to be a good friend.

WRITING PROMPTS

1. Hannah has to make a choice between hanging out with her friend or practising. Write about a time you had to make a difficult decision.

2. Hannah is nervous to try out for the school dance team. Write about a time you felt nervous. How did you overcome your nerves?

3. Caitlin gets angry when Hannah chooses practice over hanging out with her. Try writing chapter nine from Caitlin's point of view.

MORE ABOUT DANCE

If you're thinking about joining a dance team, it's important to know the basics ahead of time. Learning the different styles of dance can help you become a more well-rounded dancer.

Ballet – The classical, highly technical genre of ballet can be traced back to the 15th century and serves as the backbone for many other styles of dance. The most recognised form focuses on pointe work and flowing, yet precise, acrobatic movements.

Tap – Tap dancing involves dancers wearing special shoes with metal taps on the heel and toe. Tap dancers use their feet like percussive instruments to create patterns and beats.

Hip-Hop – Hip-hop dancing has roots in hip-hop culture and involves high-energy dancing with moves like breaking, popping, locking and krumping. Hip-hop music provides the beat for most hip-hop dancing, and the majority of dance moves are open to improvisation and personal interpretation.

Jazz – Jazz is a fun, energetic style of dance that is becoming increasingly popular as it showcases a dancer's individual style and originality. Jazz allows dancers to incorporate unique moves, fancy footwork, big leaps and quick turns into their routines. Many jazz dancers also have a ballet background, which helps with grace and balance.

THE FUN DOESN'T STOP HERE!

Discover more
Sport Stories at

www.raintree.co.uk